Daisy and the Beastie

Jane Simmons

ORCHARD

For Freyja and Oscar
and their weird parents

ORCHARD BOOKS
Carmelite House
50 Victoria Embankment
London EC4Y 0DZ

First published by Orchard Books in 2000

First paperback edition published in 2001

This edition published in 2004

ISBN 978 1 84362 274 1

Text and illustrations © Jane Simmons 2000

The rights of Jane Simmons to be identified as the author and illustrator of this book have
been asserted by her in accordance with the Copyright, Designs and Patents Act, 1988.
A CIP catalogue record for this book is available from the British Library.

3 5 7 9 10 8 6 4

Printed in China

Orchard Books
An imprint of Hachette Children's Group
Part of The Watts Publishing Group Limited
An Hachette UK Company

www.hachette.co.uk

Grandpa was just finishing Daisy's favourite story.
"...they searched the farm, but no one found
the Beastie!" he said.
"Coo," said Daisy.

Grandpa slowly closed his eyes and began to snore.
"Don't worry," said Daisy. "We'll find the Beastie!"
"Beastie," said Pip.

"The Beastie might be with the chickens,"
said Daisy.
"Cheep, cheep," chirped the chicks.
"Cheep," said Pip.

"...or hiding with the geese."
"Beep! beep!" said the goslings.
"Beep!" said Pip.

"The Beastie's not in the barn,"
said Daisy.
"Moo," said the calves.
"Baa!" said the lambs.
"Moo, baa," said Pip.

"...or in the meadow."
"Buzz," buzzed the bees.
"Buzz," said Pip.

There was no Beastie in the pig sty.
"Wee, wee," squealed the piglets.
"Wee," said Pip.

...nor in the orchard.
Hoppity hop, hop!
Just then...

...there was a noise from the shed.
"Eeooow!" it went.
"It's the Beastie!" said Daisy.
"Ooo!" said Pip.

Daisy and Pip
couldn't see anything.

As they crept forward,
something rumbled,
"MEEEE..."

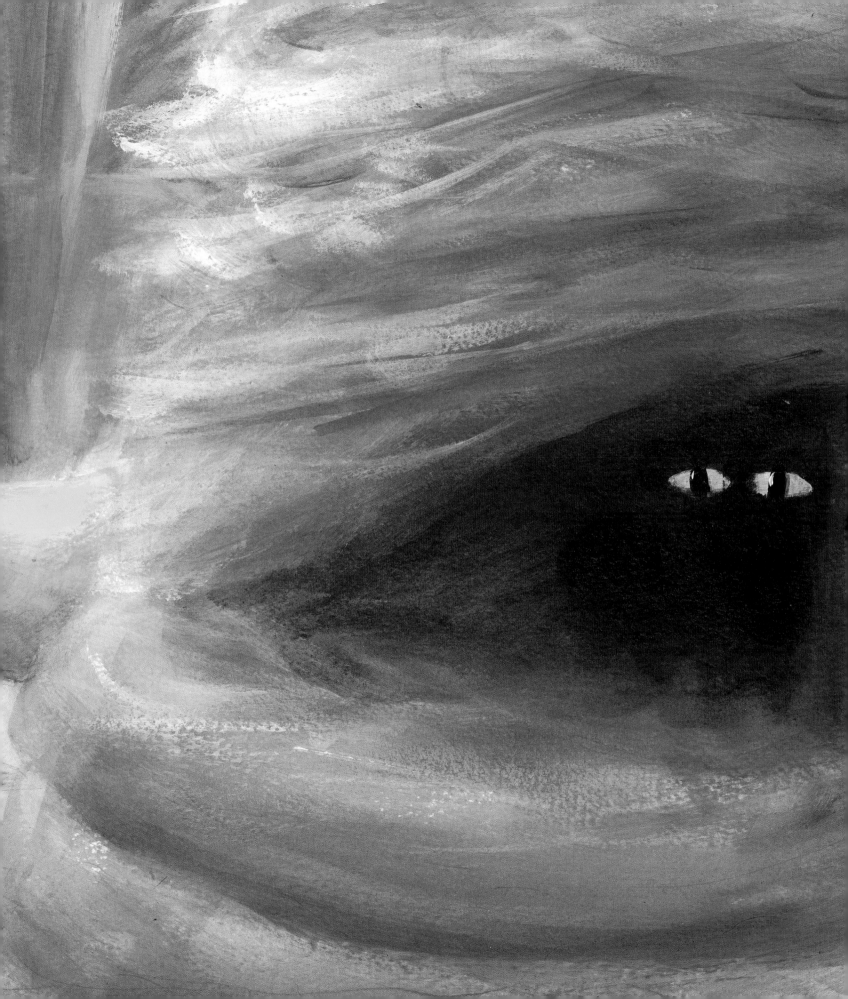

"...EEOOOW!"

"It's the Beastie! Run, Pip, run!"
cried Daisy.

"We found the Beastie!"
"The Beastie!" said Grandpa. "Where?"
"THERE!"

"Meooow," said the kittens.
"Coo," said Daisy.
"Coo," said Pip.
. Grandpa laughed...

...and Daisy and Pip played
with all the kitten beasties.